Mission Viejo Library
100 Civic Center
Mission Viejo, CA 92691
MAY 2 4 2006

Lexile 620
.3

W9-AVN-193

SIX EMPTY POCKETS

written by
Matt Curtis

illustrated by
Mary Newell DePalma

Children's Press®
A Division of Scholastic Inc.
New York Toronto London Auckland Sydney
Mexico City New Delhi Hong Kong
Danbury, Connecticut

For my young friend,
Charles Crittenden – M.N.D.

Reading Consultant
LINDA CORNWELL
Learning Resource Consultant
Indiana Department
of Education

Library of Congress Cataloging-in-Publication Data
Curtis, Matt.
Six empty pockets / by Matt Curtis ; illustrated by Mary Newell DePalma.
p. cm. — (Rookie reader)
Summary: Charles's six empty pockets come in handy for carrying such treasures as a blue star marble, an old crow's feather, and seven striped stones.
ISBN 0-516-20399-1 (lib. bdg.)—ISBN 0-516-26253-X (pbk.)
[1. Pockets—Fiction.] I. DePalma, Mary Newell, ill. II. Title. III. Series.
PZ7.C9445Si 1997
[E] —dc21

96-49441
CIP
AC

© 1997 by Children's Press®, a Division of Grolier Publishing Co., Inc.
Illustration © 1997 by Mary Newell DePalma
All rights reserved. Published simultaneously in Canada
Printed in the United States of America
4 5 6 7 8 9 10 R 06 05 04 03 02 01

Charles's favorite pants
have six empty pockets!

Charles drops a blue star marble in his right front pocket.

In his left back pocket,

he packs a
tractor-trailer truck.

In his two side pockets,
his mother slips a sandwich . . .

. . . and a sweet, golden pear.

He pokes an old crow's feather,
black and shiny in the sun,

in his left front pocket.

And for good luck,

in his right back pocket,

he stashes seven
striped stones.

After lunch . . .

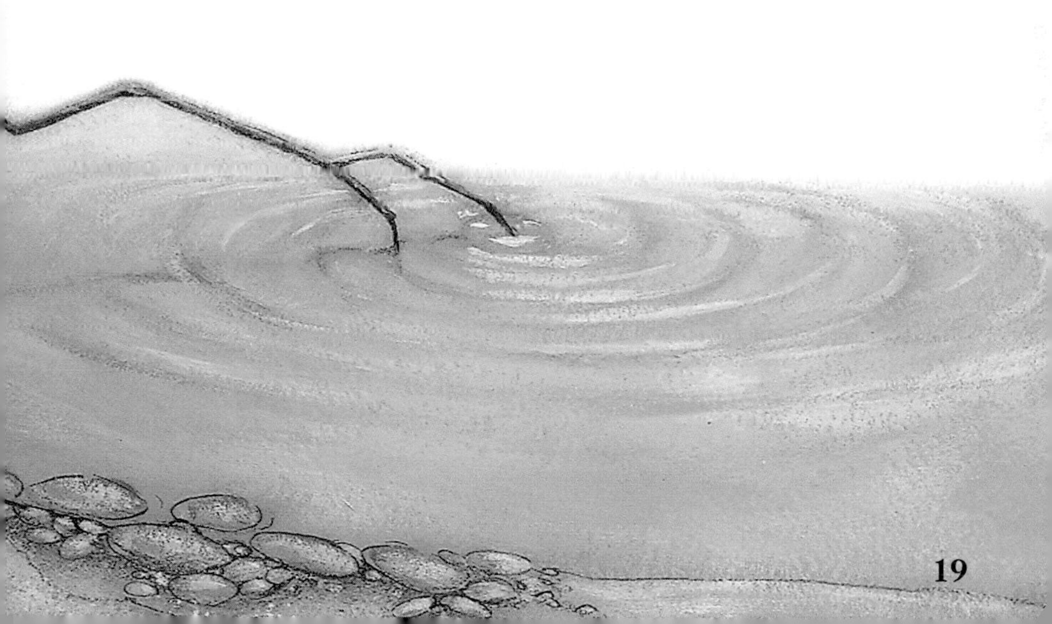

. . . he stuffs his side pockets full of seedpods from a honey locust tree.

But when Charles sees
the best prize of all,

a frog, with big,
bulging eyes,

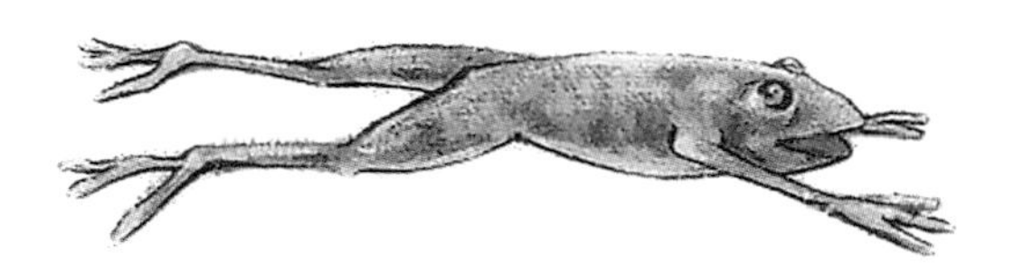

his pockets are just too full!

At night, Charles counts out his treasures and thinks about tomorrow.

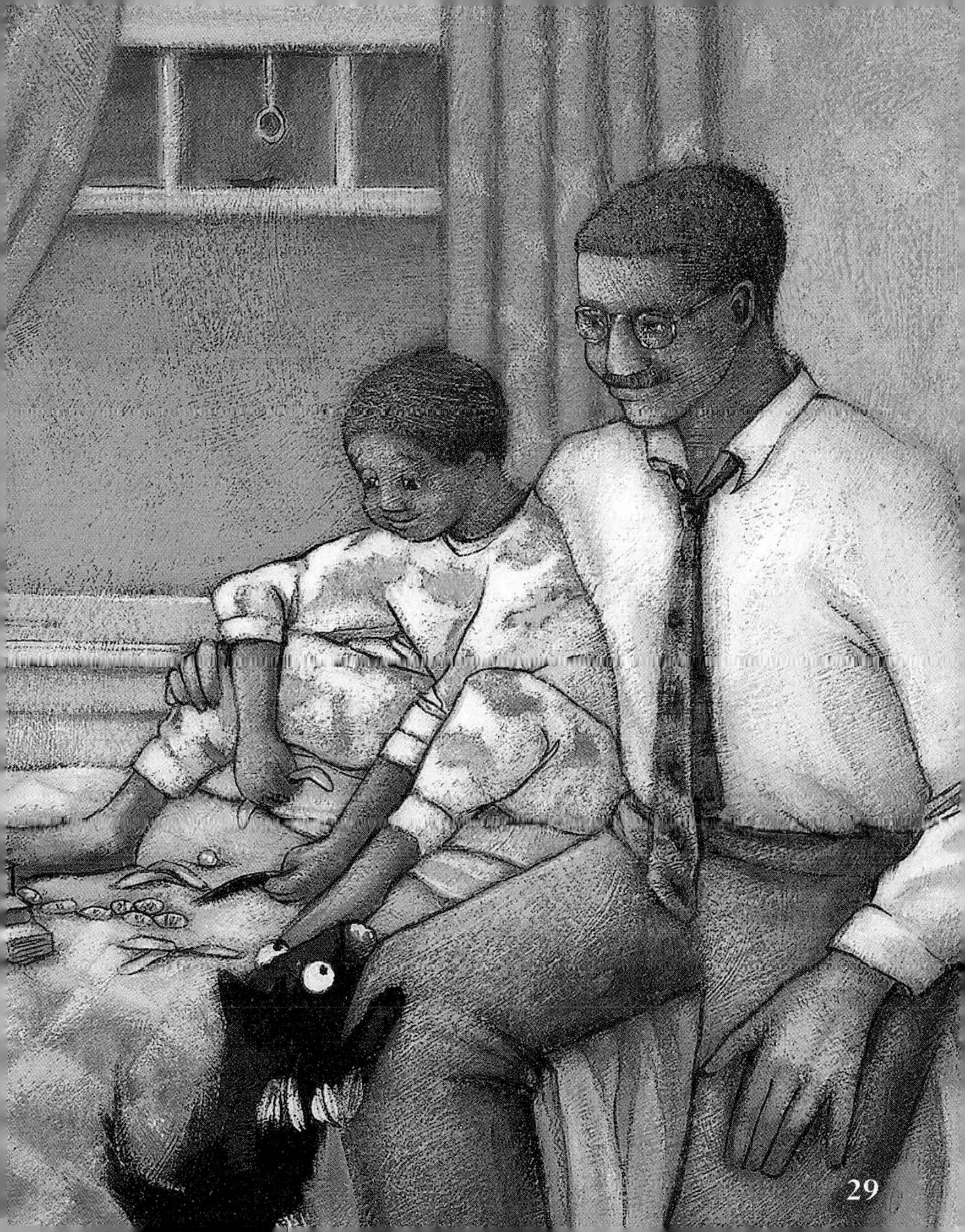

Six more empty pockets!

Word List (82 Words)

a
about
after
all
an
and
are
at
back
best
big
black
blue
bulging
but
Charles
Charles's
counts
crow's
drops
empty
eyes
favorite
feather
for
frog
from
front
full
golden
good
have
he
his
honey
in
just
left
locust
luck
lunch
marble
more
mother
night
of
old
out
packs
pants
pear
pocket
pockets
pokes
prize
right
sandwich
seedpods
sees
seven
shiny
side
six
slips
star
stashes
stones
striped
stuffs
sun
sweet
the
thinks
tomorrow
too
tractor–trailer
treasures
tree
truck
two
when
with

About the Author

Matt Curtis is a writer living in Salt Lake City, Utah.

About the Illustrator

Mary Newell DePalma works as a freelance illustrator, drawing and painting pictures for books, magazines, newspapers, and textbooks. She lives in Boston, Massachusetts, with her husband and two children.